Bridge of Love

Nana Malone

NANA
MALONE

COPYRIGHT

This is a work of fiction. Names, characters, places, and incidents either are the product of the author's imagination or are used fictitiously, and any resemblance to actual persons living or dead, business establishments, events, or locales, is entirely coincidental.

Bridge of Love

Cover Art by Minx Malone

Edited by Angie Ramey, and Michelle Ficht

Published in the United States of America

Chapter One

B ridge

I knew she was trouble the moment I saw her.

Emma Varma.

I would know that ass anywhere. The real question was, what was she doing here on campus? And how hadn't she been seen already?

Under any circumstances, a girl like Emma was going to get noticed. All that raven dark hair, silky and hanging to the middle of her back. Cinnamon skin. As much as Eton liked to purport that they accepted many underprivileged boys, there was a distinct lack of diversity. Brown skin, great ass, and long flowing hair combined to scream *girl on campus.* Usually that meant the vultures should have been circling, so how had no one seen her?

She was scurrying around the corner from Toby's room. Had she come to see him? Was something wrong with Pamma Auntie?

There was a small part of me that wished she was coming to see me.

Ha. A small part? Is that part me... your dick?

Toby Varma was one of my best mates. I'd known Emma since Toby and I started at Eton a few years ago. When I met her, she'd been knobby kneed with a dirt smudged face and very annoying.

Well, she was *still* very annoying.

I glanced over my shoulder to see that no one else had seemed to notice her, so I followed her down the back stairwell that led down to one of two study rooms. One of them, I will admit, had a secret entrance. It was one that we seniors tended to use to sneak out to go drink or head out to a party. How did Emma know about it?

I glanced down at my watch. It was four-thirty. The study rooms wouldn't be busy. There might be one or two people studying, but they might not see her.

I had to run to keep up. I checked the first study room, the small one, but she wasn't there. And then in the second, I saw her as she hit a hidden book, pulling it free and sending the shelves of books swinging.

Jesus Christ, she was a disaster everywhere she went.

I followed her quickly, glancing behind me and making sure no one was following us. *Where are you going, Ems?* I followed her into the passage where darkness hit me hard, and I had to let my eyes adjust. At the other end, I saw the light of the swinging door that led outside to the grounds. From there would be the path down to the teacher's parking lot. Below that would be the student parking lot, though it was nearly impossible to get a parking space at this time of day. On the left, there was a covered path to the equestrian arena and one to the boathouse used by the rowing team.

I followed her down the path to the boathouse and then caught up to her easily.

I knew I shouldn't scare her. But she was running around fucking Eton by herself. No escort. Wearing tight jeans and a crop top, and she was going to get in a lot of trouble, not to mention the trouble Toby could get into. Not that what she was wearing should garner any unwanted attention. She could and should wear what she wanted.

I also knew arseholes. Eton was full of them. Hell, most of them had never even seen a real live girl they weren't related to. Someone would fucking lose their shit and report her, say something shitty to her, or worse.

The idea of any of those things happening to her had my teeth grinding and my hands curling into fists.

I would end anybody who said anything to her. If anyone touched her... fuck. They would wish I killed them.

My oh-so-helpful brain replayed an image of the last time I'd lost control. The incident that had landed me at Eton as my last chance, according to the old man. Before I'd come here, I was one of those East End hooligans people saw on the news.

I never hurt anyone really, but I was in trouble a lot. Vandalism mostly. Mostly bored kid shite. Mum was working all the time to try and get the restaurant going. And I was perpetually angry at the old man I knew existed for never helping her.

Add to that I was shit bored at school and it was a recipe for disaster. It was a wonder I wasn't in jail or dead.

At any rate, this idiot bloke had tried to hurt one of my mates back home. Sweetest girl you'd ever met. Really shy. The fucker had pulled her around by her hair during an argument. So naturally, I'd called him out on his bullshit and the bloody geezer came at me with a knife.

He'd ended up on the wrong end of his own knife that night. It wasn't fatal or anything. I'd even applied pressure to his shoulder wound while holding him down so my mate could shave his head.

Okay, maybe that was a smidge too far. Point was, I wasn't going to tolerate any verbal or physical harm coming to Emma.

She was my best mate's little sister and deserved respect.

Right... and that's the only reason?

"Now where do you think you're going?"

She whirled around, ready to scream. But I pulled her against me and clamped a hand over her mouth. "Be quiet, Emma."

At first her eyes were wide and fearful, and she struggled. But when she saw it was me, her brows furrowed and dropped down. I could feel her teeth starting to graze the flesh of my palm. "Do not bite."

She blinked rapidly. Then her eyes seemed to be smiling at me, and I knew I was in trouble. As if sensing what she was going to do, my body moved automatically, one leg bending and crossing over my body to protect my balls. Emma hit the outside of my thigh, and then her teeth clamped down on my flesh.

I muttered a curse. "I fucking told you to shut up. Hold still. It's just me. Are you trying to get caught?"

That seemed to get her attention, and she relaxed and stilled.

"What are you doing here, Emma?"

She shoved at my chest, and I had no choice but to release her. "Well, if you would fucking leave me be, I could go find him."

"Are you looking for Toby?"

She rolled her eyes. "No, I was here to seduce you."

That rasp in her voice and the way her gaze landed over me with just a hint of derision drove me insane. I wasn't sure why, because fucking hell, there were a million girls I could have, a million of them who clearly wanted me.

But Emma. Fucking Emma. Every time I was near her, it was like someone set my body on fire, making my skin too warm, too tight, too itchy. I usually avoided touching her at all cost. But I had made a rookie mistake, and now my body tingled as I faced off against her.

"You turn up dressed like that on an all-boys campus and think no one is going to notice?"

"What was I supposed to do?"

"Well, if you are trying to sneak around campus, you should have hidden your hair with a hat and actually put on a uniform. Not that that would have done much to hide your ass, but it would have been less conspicuous. But instead, you went around in those tight jeans and crop top, giving the boys no choice but to stare at it as it hugs your tits. Now, I recognize that's not your intention and that there's nothing wrong with the way you're dressed. But you have to take into consideration that A, this is an all-boys campus with a lot of lads who haven't seen a girl in a long time, and B, they have no idea what to do with one, and C, they can't help but to objectify girls. And still, you're running around here as if none of that matters? That's not how life works, Ems."

She scowled then. What the fuck had I said wrong this time?

"I don't need a big brother. I have one. One who has abandoned me for the holiday. Where is he?"

I blinked. Toby had abandoned her? No fucking way. He and his family were close, like my mom and me.

7

"If you'd been caught in our room, we'd both have been expelled."

"I'm his sister. That doesn't count."

"Yes, it does. The rules are very clear. Sister, mom, or grandmother, no women allowed. We would have been expelled."

She frowned at that. "Well, how was I supposed to know?"

"You didn't really think that through, did you?"

"Whatever. Look, you're not my big brother. You're not the boss of me, so I don't care what you think. Just tell me where he is, will you?"

"Well, I'm not just going to leave you on campus to look for him alone."

"Yes, you are."

"Why?"

"Because I will make being with me a giant colossal pain in the ass. So you might as well just let me go."

I ground my teeth. "No. Let's go. He's probably at the boathouse."

"You're serious? You're going to walk me there?"

I nodded. "Yeah, because that's what Toby would want."

She rolled her eyes. "You really are never any fun. You know that, right?"

"I didn't realize fun was what you needed from me."

"It'd be nice. You know, for you *not* to be uptight and a giant colossal pain."

I shrugged. "I don't really care about being a pain in the ass."

"Yeah, clearly. It shows."

"Fine." I forced a tight smile onto my face, and she shook her head.

"You know what, it's better when you don't smile."

I couldn't help it. A smirk teased out. "So, you want to tell me what you're doing here?"

"Yeah, I'm trying to force Toby to come home."

"I mean, you know he loves you, right? If he could come home, he would."

She chewed her bottom lip. "You don't get it. We're all each other has. Mom drives me crazy, and he's the buffer. Plus, he promised me something."

"Whatever he promised you, I'm sure he'll make it up to you."

At the boathouse, I could see Toby as he prepped some equipment. "Your brother is over there."

She groaned. "Ugh, I should have just come here first. My friend dropped me off after therapy."

I squinted against the sun as I caught sight of the car on top of the hill. "You hiked all the way to campus from there?"

"Yeah, I didn't want to be seen."

I shook my head. "Wow, Emma Varma, when will you ever learn that there is an easier way to do things?"

She turned and gave me a saucy smile as she backed away from me. "Now what fun would that be? See you around, Bridge."

I forced myself to not call out after her as she turned to jog toward the boathouse. It wasn't my business. And that tingling from where I'd touched her before hadn't disappeared. This was the problem with Emma Varma. It had always been the problem. Even before I really knew or understood that whole relationship-with-girl's thing, I knew she made me insane, too hyper aware. She unsettled me, and it had gotten worse over the years as she began to grow and develop. How many times had I stayed at Toby's house with Emma constantly trying to get our attention? *My* attention. Always trying to push me. But I'd held strong. Now was not the time for a show of weakness. Even though Emma Varma had grown up, she was still way the hell off limits. My best mate's little sister? No way, no how. Forgetting about her was in my very best interest.

Toby

I was about to blow up my life.

One decision, one false move, and everything would explode. I often thought about it. If I had stepped right instead of left that day, maybe I wouldn't have even seen what happened, and I'd still be oblivious. The problem was, now there was no unseeing it. I was already ashamed of myself for holding onto the information for far too long. A part of me hoped maybe I hadn't seen what I thought I saw, that maybe I'd gotten it wrong. And when the incident hadn't shown up on the news, when no one had said a word about the girl, I had managed to somewhat convince myself of that. Except, I *had* seen it. I knew I had. So at exactly 2:00 p.m. tomorrow, if everything went right, I was going to blow up the truth. Instead of going home to London for a holiday break with my mates, I was going to stay on campus. I was going to go to the Dean of Students and tell him what I'd seen. The Dean of Students was also a member of the oh-so Elite organization. The organization that was going to determine the future of my life and of my mates' lives for that matter.

If they knew what I was going to do, would they stop me? I'd like to think not. I'd like to think that they would walk in there and stand beside me, but I wasn't going to drag them into this. If I was going to get kicked out for speaking the truth, then fair enough, but I was going to make sure that they were protected. So instead of going home, I was staying on campus. I'd already told my mum, and she was displeased. And I told my sister two days ago, as well. Emma was apoplectic. I'd promised to take her to some stupid concert by Estella Grant, some poppy, wannabe singer. Mom had said she could only go if she had an escort because Mom knew Emma well. And I was supposed to be Emma's escort. But if I was staying on campus, I couldn't be. I had found the perfect solution though. I was just going to have to live with my choice.

Emma was difficult in the best of times. I loved my sister to distraction, but she was wild and free and would ruin your whole day because you crossed your eyes at her. But she was also quick-witted and fun to be with. And at the core of it, Emma was also really compassionate. She couldn't stand to see anyone treated unfairly, and she would go full war crusader on their behalf. The problem was that Emma didn't always look before she jumped. She was the type of person who confronted right then and there about it, without even thinking of the outcome. I was always telling her to wait and think before she acted.

Just like I had waited patiently and deliberately. But I was *too* deliberate sometimes, and I had thought about this one for too long.

Maybe you didn't see what you thought you saw. Maybe everything is fine. Maybe everyone is fine.

But I could feel it in my gut. What I'd seen had been real. I hadn't imagined it. I hadn't been pissed enough to have hallucinated it. It had happened. And I knew the expectation was for me to stay quiet, stay silent. But I couldn't. Oaths or no oaths.

The only problem was that if what I'd seen had been real, everything I had worked so hard for was going to come to a screeching halt, and I was going to humiliate my father, my family, everyone.

Your father who doesn't talk to you? Who hasn't seen you or your sister since you were seven and Emma was four?

That was the thing with organizations like the Elite. Once I was initiated, I would see my father once a month, every month. He'd be behind a mask, but I would know it was him. I was his son, and he still wouldn't speak to me. He would not acknowledge me. He would still look at me like a stranger, but I would be there with him and someday be his equal.

Are you sure about that? What if he never acknowledges you?

Okay, fine. I at least *hoped* we would be equals. It didn't even have to be reconciliation, but maybe respect wasn't too much to hope for.

You're delusional.

Maybe, but either way, this information wouldn't hold any longer. I couldn't hold onto it anymore because one among us was the devil and was going to bring everything down. And he had to be stopped.

Oh yeah, like you're the one who could stop him. He has everything. The family, the connections, the pedigree. No one will believe you.

Whether people were going to believe me or not, I had to try, even if I ruined everything. I knew the right thing to do. I just had to do it.

You will destroy your life.

Well then, so be it. I would destroy my life. But at the very least, I would have done the right thing, and the poor family that might be looking for that girl would finally know the truth about what happened to her.

A shiver ran up my back as I thought about that night. The fear that I could have done more, that I should have done more. But I'd been frozen, At first unsure of what I had seen, then unwilling to believe it. The horrifying acceptance had come later.

I'd considered going to the police directly, but if I called the police to Eton with no proof, that would be a disaster. No, speaking to the dean was the better way.

I'd been distracted while I ruminated on my plan, and I froze as I saw someone with dark hair coming around the corner of the boathouse. "Emma Varma, what the fuck are you doing out here?"

"It's a boathouse. People come to row all the time."

"Yes, but it's a fucking school day, Ems. Did you sneak out?"

"Maybe?"

I glanced around, trying to figure out how the hell my sister had gotten into the boathouse. And then I noticed a car at the top of the hill, and it looked like a girl was waving down at Emma. "Oh my God, who is that?"

"That's my mate, Katy."

"Wait, Katy Finch? Didn't you get in trouble with her last term? She nearly got you expelled, Emma."

"Ugh, St. Harrow's. It's so annoying. Sister Eunice has it in for me."

"You're not supposed to be here, Ems."

"I know, I know, but to be fair, you bailed out on me. That's the reason I'm here. I need you to find me a replacement."

"A replacement?"

"You know I will die if I don't go to that concert."

"I know and I'm sorry, but it can't be avoided. I've got to stay here."

"For what? Some kind of stupid project? You weren't even clear when you told me you won't be able to make it. If you're going to lie, lie better."

I watched my sister, the setting sun kissing her skin, making it glow. "Look, I'm sorry, love, but I promise I'll make it up to you. It's just been a crazy time with everything going on here. I have to stay and finish a project, okay?"

"You're a party pooper. Mom will never let me go to that concert now. She doesn't trust Katy."

"Well, she shouldn't. Expulsion, Emma, really?"

"Like I said, Sister Eunice has it in for me."

"You mean, outside of the fact that you snuck out, stole a car, and drove forty miles to see me instead of being where you're supposed to be?"

"I'm your sister, and you love me though. And I missed you."

She bit her bottom lip and I could tell part of that was put on, but there was also truth in what Emma was saying. I stalked over to her and wrapped my arms around her. "You're such a pain in the ass. What is wrong with you?"

"Oh, nothing really. It just felt like you abandoned me."

"I have never abandoned you a day in my life, and I'm not starting now."

She wrapped her arms around me tight. "Tobes, I know you don't want to talk to me about the whole secret club and all that."

I frowned. "Ems..."

"No, I'm not saying anything. I promise. It's just... You're right here in his legacy spot and doing, you know, all the things. Becoming everything he wants you to become. And I just don't want to lose my brother."

"I hear you. And you won't, okay? I swear it on my soul; you will not lose me. And I'm not going to get caught up in him. I'm going to do what I came to do. Create a better future for you, me, and Mom. He can feel free to fuck right off."

She smiled at that. "I do like that idea. It's just... I know what it's like. How he can seem. We've both seen him before."

"I know. I know, Ems. I've got it handled."

"Well, you're more sensitive than I am. What if he manages to trick you? You know, trick you into being his son."

I laughed. "Really, Ems?"

"I don't know. It just sucks."

"I hear you. But come on, let's get you back to school. Do you want me to drive you back?"

"Then how would you get back here?"

"I could take the train."

"No, you stay where you're supposed to be. Katy will drive me back. We'll get there before curfew, I promise."

"You only have two more days until break, Ems, okay? And I promise, I'll fine you a replacement escort."

She wrinkled her nose. "Oh God, please, not Drew."

I laughed. "What's wrong with Drew?"

"Nothing's wrong with Drew. He's just so... I don't know..."

"It's not Drew."

"Okay, fine. East or Ben would be great."

I smiled at her. "I see you're making your picks on the two pretty boys."

"They're very nice to look at. I have eyeballs that work."

I rolled my eyes. "That's gross. Those are my mates."

"Yeah. Either of those two. Not Bridge."

I laughed. "You two are like oil and water. I don't know what's the matter with you."

"Well, he's a dick. So, there's that."

"Yeah, he can be a bit of a tosser. But he's a good bloke."

My sister gave me another tight squeeze. "Well, I'd better get out of here. My brother insists that I have to go and be a good citizen or some such nonsense."

I grinned. "I love you, Ems."

"I love you too, Tobes."

I watched as she hustled back up the hill. She was not going to be thrilled when she found out her escort for the night was Bridge. Ben was off on a vacation with his family, and East couldn't make it. So Bridge had to be the one. But she would find out soon enough, and Bridge would look after her.

I just hoped he'd be able to handle my sister. These days, Emma was unpredictable at best, so he'd have to have a firm hand and make sure she didn't run all over him. But I could trust him to look after her while I blew up my life.

Chapter Two

Bridge

"Mate, would you hold up?"

I knew what was coming. I'd taken steps to avoid it, but I hadn't been quick enough.

Hearing Toby's voice was enough of a warning. Hell, seeing Emma this afternoon had been my warning. She'd been hell bent on seeing her brother and getting some answers about why he was ditching her for the holiday.

Call it a premonition, a foreshadowing, or just bad luck. Either way, one of my best mates was going to ask for the one favor I couldn't give. To look out for his little sister over the holiday. Sadly, I knew I was the only choice. I was the only one going home for the holiday. Our other mates were going off on family vacations.

I loved Toby. He was the best mate a bloke could ask for. But this favor? Just no. It couldn't be done. For starters, Emma was a giant pain in the arse, and everyone knew it. She was just on the cusp of wild child, and I knew for a fact she was a handful. Secondly, she had daddy issues, which meant she wanted to take them out on every bloke who dared to look at her cross-eyed.

Third, and perhaps the most pressing issue of all...

I wanted her.

More than I'd probably ever wanted anything in my life. Hence, why me being anywhere near her was a terrible idea.

Toby was looking for someone upstanding to look out for her, and that wasn't me.

"Sorry, mate, I've got to catch the train home."

Unlike the rest of my classmates, I didn't have a parent there to pick me up at Eton. Toby was staying for the holiday because he had a project going that he needed to keep an eye on. He'd tried to explain it to me, but once the science nerd part of him came out, I'd stopped listening.

Toby was the kind of mate that everyone needed. Affable, kind at the core. I'd never met anyone like him. "Tobes, you have that look on your face. I've got to go, or I'll miss my train. Ben's car is giving me a lift to the station."

He frowned then. "You're not going home with Ben?"

"They offered to drive me, but for them to go all the way to East London with traffic, you know how it is. Besides, they have a late flight to catch to St. somewhere or other."

Toby frowned. He knew how it was. Neither one of us particularly liked taking charity from our mates. It was almost better to be left to it than to be driven all the way back to London in a Rolls Royce, knowing full well that our fathers *could* provide but chose not to.

"Yeah, mate, I get it. Okay look, it's just a small favor. Why do you have that look on your face?"

All around us, in the cobblestones and stone parapets of Eton, stood hundreds of years of tradition and power, all contained in these walls. A sea of gray and navy blue floated around as students hustled to head home for the holiday. There were a few students who changed into their street clothes before going home, but even those were versions of the Eton uniform.

Suit. Trousers. A watch that would have fed my family for months.

I rolled my eyes. *Money.*

I hadn't changed, simply because it would have required more time. I just wanted out of the prison. I was in a hurry to put distance between the place that promised me a future with strings and my past.

Also, I wasn't too eager to stick around on the off chance my father *did* show, which was extremely unlikely. But still, he'd come before, and it hadn't been pleasant. I knew Toby was going to stand there until I gave in, so I sped up the process. "What do you need, mate?"

His grin flashed, warming up his dark eyes. "It's not so bad. Will you chill? I only need you to keep an eye on Ems for one night."

She was possibly the hottest girl I had ever seen in my life. All dark hair, dark brown skin, melting enormous topaz eyes that looked like a banked fire. The kind of things that give you months of dreams that you shouldn't have about your best mate's sister.

He continued pushing me into agreeing. "Look, I wouldn't ask, but I'm not going home. She's supposed to go to some concert. Some hip-hopper, pop star, whatever. I have a ticket. Would you just go keep an eye on her and keep her out of trouble? She's got some new friends, and I don't know what they're like. She's been looking forward to this, and I was supposed to go with her. If you could just do me this favor, I'd be a mate for life."

I shook my head. "Toby, no. Your sister, she's trouble. Pure fucking mischief. Do you remember that last time I stayed with you? She got into her mum's knickers with that friend of hers. What was her name again?"

Toby sighed. "Katy. You see why I'm worried? She's heading off to this concert with Katy. Come on, mate. I wouldn't ask if I didn't have to. I was supposed to go and keep an eye on them, and now that I'm staying here, I can't. So please, be a mate."

I couldn't say, *Mate, every time I'm near your sister, I keep picturing sliding my tongue into her mouth and feeling her tits that are far too big for such a skinny little thing and making her purr my name.*

Nope, those were not things you said to your best mate.

Behind us, I could hear Ben's low mumble. "What's the holdup, princess?"

I rolled my eyes. "Me and you, who's the princess?"

Ben grinned then. *Ben Covington*, the fair-haired Viking, except more English than the lot of us. He was all bleach-blond waves, broad smile, big shoulders. I was as tall as he was, but I was leaner. And I was the dark-haired devil to his sun-licked Viking god. But he was another one of my best mates. And behind him came East Hale. Broad smile, laptop bag strapped over his shoulder, clutching on to it like it was his passport to the good life. "What the fuck is the holdup, mate?"

I rolled my eyes. "Nothing's the holdup. Time to go."

But Toby wasn't letting me go that easily. "I'm just trying to get Bridge here to agree to do me a favor when he's at home."

East rolled his eyes, ribbing him gently. "Mate, I'm not sure why you like the dirty magazines, there's porn on the internet. It's free. You don't have to make Bridge buy them for you."

A flush crept over Toby's face even as he flipped East off. East, the twat, just grinned. He may have been all geeked out, but somehow he managed to give off a lad's-lad vibe. And he was actually all right. I'd never really expected to like him that much. But these three and Drew Wilcox, they were my best mates. The ones that stuck around when the shit went haywire. Drew had already left for home. He had also offered to drive me, but again, I didn't like handouts. And his father had actually come to pick him up, and the last thing I needed was all sorts of questions on where my father was and what our family was doing for the holiday and if I was going to be at a ball or a gala or a society function. Questions that he already knew the answers to. My father was a friend of his. Why didn't he just ask the old man?

Nope, better to avoid questions. Better to avoid too many entanglements.

Unfortunately, no one told Toby this.

"I'm just taking a shot at Bridge here to agree to look out for Emma at the concert she's going to."

East perked up. "I could go to the concert."

Toby shook his head. "No, you are not to touch my fucking sister."

East held his hands up. "Mate, I'm wounded. I wouldn't touch your sister."

This was a lie of course. Toby rolled his eyes. "Not with your hands. You'd use your mouth. No fucking way."

East just smirked, because as nerdy as he was, he'd researched a hundred ways to make a girl come with nothing more than his mouth. It was worrisome to think about if you had a sister.

Ben shrugged. "I'll do it."

All three of us laughed then.

Toby rolled his eyes. "What, you, pretty boy? No. When Emma was here last time, all she was talking about was how insanely pretty you are. Nope, you're not going anywhere near my sister."

Ben frowned. "I wouldn't touch her."

Toby's laugh was a low chuckle. "I'm not worried about *you* touching *her*. Emma would eat you alive. You're not ready for that. You're still a virgin."

Ben scowled at him.

"It's all right, mate, it's true. But Bridge... Bridge can handle himself. And he is the least affected by anything out of all of us." Toby turned back to me. "Just do it," he begged.

"Why the fuck won't you just say you'll do it so we can get on the road? I don't want to stay at school any longer than necessary," Ben growled.

The way they were watching me expectantly, I knew what I was going to have to say, and none of it was going to be appropriate. And whatever I said was going to piss Toby the fuck off. Normally, I didn't care about pissing people off, but this was Tobes. He never asked for anything as a general rule. So I was in no kind of mood.

"Fuck me. Fine. Text me the ticket info, but honest to fucking God, I'm not partying afterward. I'm just getting her out of there and making sure she gets home all right, yeah?"

Toby nodded.

Chapter Three

Bridge

"You know, sooner or later he's going to figure it out."

I slid my gaze over to Ben as we rolled toward the train station. "Figure what out?"

His chuckle was low, even as he rolled his eyes. "That you have the hots for Emma."

How the fuck did he know? My brow furrowed. "I don't have the hots for Emma. She's Toby's little sister. Nothing is going to happen there."

"Oh come on, you know Toby wouldn't be like that. You're his mate. He'd be happy if you're the one that goes out with Emma."

"Something tells me that isn't true."

His grin flashed. "What, you would rather East date her?"

"If East puts his fucking hands on her, mate or no mate, I will kill him."

"Oh right, and you don't feel anything for her at all."

He has a point there, you wanker.

I rolled my eyes. "It doesn't matter what I feel. Nothing's going to happen."

"Look, I saw it the last time we all went home with Toby on holiday. It's only a matter of time until he sees it too. All I'm saying is that it will be better if you tell him than if he sees it for himself. Which he will."

I was in no mood for rationality as the car lulled us back and forth. "Nah, mate, I got it."

"If you say so, but it's written all over your face. Do you know what you're going to do when you see her?"

"Nothing. She's annoying. A total pain in the arse. Plus, she's spoiled. A total princess who thinks the world revolves around her, or that it should. And sorry, but I don't deal with princesses."

"Right. You don't deal with princesses. Mate, this whole taking you to the train station thing, it's ridiculous. Let me drive you home. I know that you get sensitive about this, but really, be reasonable. Besides, your mum won't like it if you take the train. I honestly don't like it that you're on your own."

"Have you already talked to her?"

Ben shrugged. "I might have reached out and extended an invitation for you to come with me on holiday."

I was going to kill him. "What the fuck, mate? Didn't I tell you no already?"

"Yeah, yeah. You told me that you need to go look in on her. But I happen to know that she doesn't need looking in on. She'll be working anyway, so what are you going to do?"

Ben's car smelled of newly polished leather, and the heat in the back sunk into my bones, making me loosen up a little bit. It was so tempting to let him just drive me home, to accept the olive branch, to accept the friendship. But while I didn't really have to look in on my mum, there were other things I had to do. I didn't want Ben seeing any of that, so I held fast. "Mate, I appreciate it, but you know how it is. Sometimes I just need to tend to myself."

Ben's ice-blue gaze met mine, and there was a wisdom about his eyes that I didn't always pay attention to. While Ben seemed, on occasion, like the impulsive one among us, like the one most likely to say the wrong thing or to fuck up, he was also, next to Toby, the heart of the group. He somehow understood things way beyond his years, and he just nodded at me. "All right, I'll do what you want, but one of these days, you'll realize you don't have to do everything by yourself."

Yeah, I knew he believed that. I knew that deep down Ben believed the words he said. But while he was the son of a lord and had grown up around all the wealth and trappings that came with the title, I was only a bastard son.

I grew up on the wrong side of town and worked hard to shed my East London accent when I started going to school at Eton, where the crowd mostly thought I didn't belong. God knew my fucking father didn't think I belonged anywhere. Especially not anywhere he might run in to me or see me or have to deal with me. Ben and I had completely different upbringings. Toby wouldn't want someone like me for his sister. Emma Varma smelled clean and fresh, like linens off the line. Her eyes always held a glint of mischief, as if she knew what I was thinking, what I was so desperate to have from her, and she wanted to tease me with it. But she was forever out of reach. And she would remain that way, because while my mates knew what friendships meant, they didn't know that they were how you survived. At least where I was from.

"I appreciate it, mate. How about this... We'll compromise. You can drive me all the way back to Eton after the holiday. I'll ring you, and you can pick me up."

I was always surprised at the simple joy Ben got in doing something to help. As much as he seemed like the-devil-may-care one of the group, if it came down to one of us needing something, he was the first one to call. Because if he said he was going to do something, you could damn well guarantee he was going to make it happen.

"Mate, that's good news. Fine, then I won't take it so personally that you won't let me drive you home. Whatever you do, take care. You do that, then I'll pick you up and we'll go back to school together. Besides, you know what we're waiting on."

The pit of my stomach balled.

Oh yes, the summons from the Elite. There were the Pops, and then there were the Elite, the secret societies of Eton. If were called up from the Pops for the Elite, our lives would change. Ben, East, and Drew were already chosen. Their fathers were Elite. Toby and I were different. Our fathers were Elite, but we were their bastard children that they didn't want to see or look at or acknowledge. So it was a question whether or not we would get our summons.

Being in the Elite meant seeing my father. Which would be an issue. Why my father would deny me, God only knew. But he could certainly try to stop me from getting in. He might not stop me though. He might just make it so uncomfortable that I didn't *want* to be there. But I knew what the Elite could afford me. The money to look after my mum, the freedom and the power so that no one could look down on me again, and I could actually help people. No offense to my lads, but most of them had never had to struggle a day in their lives except for Toby.

"We'll see what happens."

As the driver pulled over at the train station, I popped the latch of the door and Ben leveled a gaze on me. "If you don't want to be Elite, you don't have to be. But no matter what, we're mates for life. But if all of us were in it together? Imagine what we could do, who we could be. Not who our fathers want us to be, but who *we* want to be. Just think about it."

"You know, when you say it with that kind of confidence, I believe you. We could be our own lords."

His smile was quick on that one. "We could be the London Lords. A new generation who doesn't give a fuck. We don't have to follow their fucking rules. You just think about it, and text me when you're ready to go back to Eton. Our future awaits."

I glanced over to the train. "Our future awaits." And mine certainly didn't involve Emma Varma.

Chapter Four

Emma

Bridge Edgerton was the most stuck-up, uptight pain in the arse I'd ever met in my life. He was also one of my brother's best mates. But God, he was just so annoying. He was one of those blokes that always seemed to be doing the right thing. Always seemed to have the right answers and know what you *should* be doing.

I loathed him.

No, you don't. You think he's sexy.

Okay, in my defense, he did have very nice shoulders. But that was hardly anything to get all worked up about. Lots of blokes had nice shoulders.

Sure, but he has nice shoulders, a jaw carved out of stone, and insane abdominal muscles.

There was no point arguing with myself, he was well fit. I saw it when he went with us on a holiday to Spain last year. His lips were so pouty I fantasized about them. But that was beside the point. The point was I couldn't stand him. And it seemed that the feeling was mutual. So what the hell was he doing at the Hive?

My mates and I had come for the Estella Grant special holiday concert. I'd been looking forward to this for *months*. I'd told Toby about it, and something told me my brother was the reason I saw Bridge Edgerton here at the Hive. Toby had bailed on me for some school project, so he'd no doubt sent Bridge there to watch me.

The Hive was one of London's largest music spots. Record execs would bring their up-and-coming talents there to showcase them. It was also a great spot for current talents. It was a smaller venue, so fans could hear the artists better. I begged Mum to let me come. I'd begged and begged, and when she finally said yes, I'd been thrilled and ecstatic. But I hadn't planned on fucking Bridge Edgerton being there.

My mate, Arabella, leaned over. "Isn't that one of your brother's mates?"

I refused to look at him. What was the point. All that fitness burned the eyes. "Nope, I don't know what you're talking about."

Arabella laughed. "Um, the bloke from last summer. The one we spent half the time staring at and the other half wishing he would just take his shirt off already. That one?"

When in doubt, lie. "No, I didn't see him. It must have been your imagination."

Arabella lifted a brow. "Come off it. Are you guys fighting?"

"For your information, I am not fighting with him. I wouldn't give Bridge Edgerton the time of the day." *Lies.* "He's a colossal pain in the arse."

Okay, that was true.

"I swear I saw him. Besides, he's perfect. What's wrong with you? Are you still going to pretend you don't like him?"

"I'm not pretending. He's a wanker." And I knew that to be a fact. Last summer, a few of the girls and I had perhaps gotten into Mum's scotch. The stuff she saved just for visitors, which was pointless, really, because she rarely ever had anyone come over.

We got into it with Bridge when he caught us having fun in the pool in Spain. He'd just been so disapproving. Threatened to grass on us if we didn't stop immediately.

Although... There was something just a little bit hot about his disapproving glare. The one that said he wanted to give me a spanking or something.

"No, love, I swear it's him. Maybe he's just here to enjoy the concert."

"Do you think he would be at any concert, let alone one by someone the media is calling the next Amy Winehouse? He's not that cool. He's just not."

Arabella laughed. "He could be. He just needs someone to loosen him up a bit."

"There is no amount of loosening up that makes some egos even mildly tolerable. You know this."

She laughed. "If you say so. I don't know why you can't just admit that you like him."

"Because I *don't* like him. Remember what I said earlier about him being a complete and total wanker?"

"Yes, yes, I know. He came down on us pretty hard for the drinking last summer, but we were drinking underage. And if your mum had found out, she would have been ticked. So in a weird way, he was looking out for us."

As it turned out we didn't have to wait long for confirmation. The crowd was like the Red Sea parting for him as his tall, lean frame pushed through. He had that long, commanding stride, and his face was set in a grim mask. When he reached us, my traitorous friends, especially Arabella, smiled and preened.

"Hey, you're that bloke from Spain last year, right?" Arabella fluttered her lashes at him.

I just rolled my eyes. "What are you doing here, Edgerton? I didn't think you were a fan of Estella."

"Well, there's a lot you don't know about me, Varma."

"If you say so. How much did my brother pay you to come and spoil my fun?"

"Toby didn't have to pay me. I'd ruin your day for free."

I scowled at him. "You know, you're such a pain in the arse. What is it you want exactly?"

He tilted his head back, muttered something to himself, and then sighed before leveling his gaze on me again. "Toby wanted to make sure you kept out of trouble. It seems like *Estella* can wind up a crowd."

"Oh my God, I don't need a governess. Is that what you are today? You're my nanny?"

He leaned in close, making sure that only I could hear his words. "It depends. Do you need a spanking?"

Okay look, I'm as feminist as the next girl. I wasn't down for being told what to do, what I could and couldn't do with my body, who I could be with, or who I could see. None of that interested me. But something about the way Bridge Edgerton said *spanking* made my lady parts tingle.

"No thanks. I'm not into it. Honestly, you can't be here just to babysit me."

He grinned then. "No. I'm also babysitting this group of infants you call your mates."

Arabella frowned. "Oh, I don't need an older brother. You don't have to babysit me."

"If you're with Emma, you're my responsibility tonight. I'll secure the drinks, all non-alcoholic, of course."

Everyone groaned. "Jesus Christ, Bridge, you're ruining the mood," I muttered.

"You're all underage. You think I'm going to let this group of pervs buy drinks for underage girls in hopes of getting somewhere with them?"

I grabbed his elbow and tugged him aside. "Oh my God, please stop. Whatever Toby is paying you, I will double it."

He chuckled. "Double it, huh?"

"Yes. Anything just to make you go away."

"Oh, I'm not going away, Emma. I'm here to make good on my word. So you and I, we're going to enjoy this concert. Together."

"And if I'm here meeting someone?"

"Well, I guess he'll have to get used to me too. But just who the fuck are you meeting?"

My brows snapped down. "None of your business."

"Tonight, it is my business."

"You wish it was your business," I spat back. I knew what we looked like. A squabbling couple.

The muscle in his jaw ticked. "Look, I don't want to be here just as bad as you don't want me here. But I gave Toby my word. So, how about you and your mates enjoy the concert and don't get up to anything wild. I'll make sure you lot get home. That's it. I'll just be right here, acting as your silent bodyguard. Does that work?"

I scowled at him. "You know I hate you."

"You know what? You are not the first person to tell me that."

"I don't believe that I would be. Seriously, just please don't say anything. Don't ruin anything for me."

The corner of his lips tipped up and smirked. "I wouldn't dream of ruining your special date. Nope, might as well settle in. It's going to be a rough ride tonight."

"I hate you."

"The feeling is mutual. Believe me, Emma, if I could be anywhere else tonight, I would be. But your brother asked me to do him a favor, so let's try not to kill each other, shall we?"

I knew that was going to be easier said than done.

Chapter Five

Bridge

Emma was trying to kill me.

It was the only explanation. Every time I turned around, she was dancing far too close to some bloke. I kept telling myself it was none of my bloody business. All I cared about was fulfilling a promise. I'd come here to watch out for her. She was mostly dancing and having fun with her mates. But the sharks were circling, and I could see them.

One in particular had joined the group of girls in the middle of the concert. They'd all hugged him like they knew him, so I hadn't complained too much, just sat at the bar, sipping my pint. It wasn't until Emma started dancing with him, all the while over his shoulders eye-fucking me, that she started to get to me.

The fuck was she playing at? I didn't have time for games. And the kind of games I want to play with her were probably not on the brother-approved list.

I gritted my teeth, and just sipped my drink, staring right back at her.

I said nothing when he put his hands on her arms. I just let the irritation boil. I said nothing when he started dry humping her on the floor in full view of everyone. I just kept sipping my damn pint. But when he dragged her into the back toward the bathrooms, there was no way I could sit and do nothing. I slammed my glass down and stood.

One of her friends came over to me. "I wouldn't go back there if I were you."

"Excuse me?"

"Back there with Emma and Anders."

"Oh Christ, his name is bloody Anders?"

"Yes. He's a mate from school."

I lifted a brow. Her brother would want me to interrupt.

Her friend—Arabella was it?—just rolled her eyes. "You're not her brother."

"Damn straight I'm not."

And then her sharp gaze narrowed on mine. "Oh, so it's like that?"

I crossed my arms. "Like what?"

I scanned the crowd, hoping to see them. When I couldn't find them, I started to move.

But Arabella was hot on my heels. "You like her."

"Nope. She's my mate's little sister. I can't like her."

"When has that ever stopped anyone?"

"It stops the good ones. I'm looking out for her. That's all."

I beat my way through the crowd. If Arabella thought she could follow, she was welcome to try.

Surprisingly she stayed hot on my tail like glue. "Then why are you just creepily stalking her? Why don't you just ask her out?"

"Because you don't ask out your best mate's sister. It's a recipe for disaster."

"Oh, this is rich. I get it now. Why Emma was so intent on bringing Anders tonight. Normally, she loathes him."

I turned around and frowned. "What are you on about?"

The music thumped. I leaned close to hear her better. "Anders. She doesn't like him. At all. She said he's a creepy, handsy arsehole. But he was the ticket hookup, so he said he was coming with us. Normally she ignores him. But it's you, isn't it? She wants to make you crazy."

"She knows better. She's not that dumb."

Arabella's grin was sweet. Sweeter than her dark makeup and barely there outfit suggested. "Then you don't know women very well. If you're not into her, I promise you Emma can take care of herself. She'll get Anders off her ass. But if you *are* into her, I think they went into the unisex bathroom back there."

Fury pumped through my blood, and I wasn't even sure why. She should honestly know better. Blokes were a handful at the best of times. What was she thinking?

I told myself it wasn't my business who the fuck Emma decided she wanted to get off with. Not my business at all.

Except Toby made it your business.

Why had he made it my business? This was just torture.

I couldn't have her because Toby was a mate. And she knew that. So she was deliberately torturing me.

Now I was going to teach her a very important lesson about how not to tease caged animals.

I fought my way through the crowd of people waiting for the loo.

When I came up to the unisex one, I shoved aside a bloke with two girls waiting with him.

"I'm going in. Try not to make a nuisance of yourself, when I do."

He grumbled but backed off as the other girls sized me up. I knew what they saw when they looked at me. I had the clothes, the look. A bit of posh. Except I *wasn't*. I'd worked hard to lose that East London accent. Worked hard so that none of my former self showed.

And Emma was about to bring all of that to the floor.

I banged on the door, but there was no answer.

The bloke behind me shrugged. "Tough call, mate. Who's in there?"

"Someone who shouldn't be."

He chuffed. "Sorry mate. Your girlfriend?"

"No, dammit. She's not my girlfriend."

"Right. So you're just trying to break into a locked bathroom for no good reason?"

When I heard a thud in the room, I immediately stopped giving a shit. I reached in my back pocket for the lock pick set I always carried with me. Especially when I was home. It was a dumb habit. I didn't need it anymore. I didn't do that sort of thing anymore.

Yeah you do.

But only when it's important.

Sure. If you have to tell yourself that.

It was quick work to open the door. And then I found Anders all over Emma. He had her lifted up onto the bathroom sink, and he was busy trying to shove her skirt up. She was fighting, pushing him away. Our gazes met over his shoulder, and her eyes were wide with panic. That was fear in her eyes.

I was going to fucking kill him.

I wish I could say I thought through my next steps very carefully, thought through my deeds. Weighed them against what it could cost me. But I didn't. Me, the always carefully crafted one who thought through everything, I didn't even think. I didn't blink. I didn't breathe. I just moved.

I closed the door behind me and grabbed him by the neck. He choked and fought me. "Oi, mate. What the fuck?"

But I was unwilling to listen to any of that bullshit. "The girl's not interested."

"What the fuck do you mean?"

He tried to square off against me, but I was bigger and meaner. He just didn't know it yet.

"This girl, she's not yours to touch."

"The fuck. She's—" My hand balled into a fist and went sailing right for his mouth before he could even get the words out. I hit him once. Good old biology rewarded me with blood spurting everywhere.

Emma gasped from the sink.

I glanced back at her. "Are you okay?"

I didn't get an immediate response so I asked again, still with a hand on poor Anders. "I can't hear you. I need to keep an eye on him so I need you to use your words. Are you okay?"

Her words were stilted, but she muttered, "Yes. Y-Yes, I'm fine."

"Good. Now go back outside with your friends. Close the door behind you."

"Bridge it's okay. I'm okay."

"You are not okay. And I'm going to impart on Anders here how that's a fucking problem for me. Now be a good girl. Off you get."

I could tell she hesitated because the door didn't open. The music remained muffled and silent. Finally, finally I heard it open, and I could breathe freely, knowing that she wasn't going to see me do everything I was capable of doing. When once again the banging noise of Lil' Wayne was muffled, I turned to the bloke who'd had his hands up Emma's skirt. "Now, you and I are going to have a little talk about just what the word no means. And it's going to be a long talk, so you probably want to buckle in for it."

Chapter Six

Bridge

I was about to break our deal.

My father and I, we'd come to a truce.

I would leave behind the life that I'd previously led. No more running around with the lads he didn't approve of and nearly getting myself killed more than once. I would walk away from all of that, and he would put me into Eton, as befitting of a son he didn't want. But I would get the opportunity and access to the kinds of people I would never have known.

I would be educated, and while I wouldn't get my due, I would get an opportunity to stick it to him. An opportunity to show that I wasn't a waste of time. An opportunity to be better, to be different.

Fuck me. I wanted to break our deal right now. I wanted to take every single skill that I had learned fighting on the streets and use them.

Once the door to the loo closed, I was willing to put my future in danger because of *her*.

Fucking Emma Varma.

But this arsehole had been trying to hurt her.

"Mate, didn't anyone ever tell you not to touch what wasn't yours?"

His eyes went round. "Mate, it's not what it looked like. She asked me in here. She was putting it all out there. And then we got started. She likes it a bit rough, you see."

"You are a vile piece of gobshite. Now, I need you not to scream because this is going to hurt. And I'd rather not get interrupted once I begin, *you see*. I'd like you to think thoroughly, directly, without dispatch. So you're going to take it, and you're going to deal with it. Do you understand?"

He shook his head back and forth. As he backed up, smashing into the wall, he put his hands out as if that was going to ward me off.

Pure rage flowed through my system, it was unlike anything I'd ever felt before in my life. Every single dodgy, back-alley encounter I'd ever experienced had led me to this.

Before, I'd fought to survive. But this? This would be for fun. He'd put his hands on Emma, so that meant he was going to die. And I was going to be the one to deliver the justice.

Quietly, I unsnapped my shirt sleeves, the button down being something that I'd seen one of the lads wearing, some designer type. I'd found a knockoff in Camden Market. It was close enough to the real thing that, unless you looked, you wouldn't notice.

I rolled up the sleeves, and then with ease, I made the familiar fist. The one that I'd been taught in the martial arts classes that were meant to soothe the rage inside me and not make me more violent. And then I fisted my left hand in his T-shirt. "It's a pain in the arse if I have to go through your lips to get to your teeth. But if you just present them, it's easier to knock them the fuck out."

"No. No, no, no. God, please God, no."

I caged the rage inside. Because I knew that if I didn't, the job wouldn't be efficient. It was going to be sloppy, and I didn't like sloppy or messy.

I released my fist, and then he howled. His head snapped back, and blood gushed out of his nose. Something cracked in the wall behind him.

With a strong hand, I waited. It was better when they begged first.

"Fuck. No, no, no. God, no. I'll never do it again. I'll leave her alone. I didn't know she was yours."

Snap. Another pop. I was finding that the more I hit him, the more dispassionate I could become. I never had a father around to teach me not to put your hands on women. It was something I just knew. It was wrong.

Pop.

"Fuck." He started to weep then, sobbing and sputtering.

It was the sobbing and sputtering that really got to me. And then that carefully leashed control on my rage slipped just a little. I released his shirt and delivered a left hook, swinging my arm wide and connecting with his cheekbone. His head smacked to the side with a crack. There was more crying.

And more hitting. More fists. More blood. It was as if I was watching myself calmly deliver the blows that would undo him. Like he had planned to undo Emma.

And then suddenly, there was a voice calling my name, and it sounded like the sweetest lullaby. "Bridge. Bridge, I'm okay. Bridge."

It was only after another three or four blows that I realized that it wasn't a lullaby but a voice. *Emma's voice.*

I turned around, and there she was in the doorway staring at me, mouth open and staring at the arsehole who'd tried to hurt her.

"I told you to get out, Emma."

"Let's go. Someone called the Bill. You're going to be arrested."

With those words, she was the cold slap I needed. "Fuck."

"Let's go." She grabbed my hand and tugged me outside, leaving Anders to slide down the wall.

"Jesus fucking Christ."

The crowd was packed in. In the hallway, it was wild. I kept my head down and tucked so no one could get a clear look at me. All they'd be able to say was that it had been some tall prick, but lucky for me, I knew the bouncers. Tommy O'Rourke once lived in my neighborhood. We were good and tight. When I brushed through the door, he gave me a nod. The corner of his lips sort of turned up into a smile. "I see you're still up to the same old tricks."

"Not sure what you're talking about."

He gave me a smirk before saying, "Go that way. Bill's coming from the other direction."

I gave him a nod of thanks and let Emma tug me down the alley away from the club. "Jesus, Bridge. What in the world were you doing?"

I tugged my hand free from hers. "What did you think I was doing?"

"You could have really hurt him."

"Yeah, that was the plan."

"You could have gone to the nick."

"I wasn't going to jail."

"Bridge, you would have killed him."

"Would I? Why would you care?"

"You have a stick up your arse, but you don't want to hurt anybody. You're Mr. Cool, Calm and Collected. You never have any emotions."

I stopped. "What?" Couldn't she see the depths of what I was trying to hold back for her? Because of her?

We went through the alley and to the other side of street. There were bars and restaurants all around us, and I said, "Look, let's get you a taxi and get you home."

"Me? We have to get *you* home. You probably need to wash your hands."

I glanced down at the blood on them and reached into my pocket and pulled out a handkerchief.

Her brows knitted. "A handkerchief?"

The bite of the cold wind whipped through my shirt. "Time to go, Ems."

"No." She held her ground.

She tugged me to the public garden where there was a coffee stand and behind that, to the left, a water fountain. She stopped, and I let her take my hand and rinse it under the ice-cold water. But I didn't even feel it. All I could feel were her soft hands on mine.

"Why did you do that, Bridge?"

She lifted her gaze to meet mine. And she had me gripped, locked into position. Unable to move or think or do anything. "Don't you know?"

She shook her head. "No. I don't know."

"I would have been destroyed if he'd hurt you. I needed to make sure he was never going to hurt you again."

"Why do you even care?"

"You know why I care."

Emma Varma was in my blood. She was under my skin, and there was no stopping it. But I couldn't tell her that because of her brother. I wasn't good enough. "Never mind. It doesn't matter. Let's get you in a cab."

But then Emma, true to form, lifted her chin and stared me down. "I'm not moving from here until you talk to me. I need to hear the words, Bridge Edgerton. Why would you do that for me?"

Instead of answering, I did the thing that I'd been trying to avoid doing. In the absence of being able to use my words to tell her how I felt, I kissed her.

Chapter Seven

Emma

I didn't know why, but I expected Bridge to taste like beer or liquor or, at the very least, sin.

But he tasted fresh and clean, like mint and something so decadent that I couldn't stop. Okay...he tasted a little like sin and bad decisions.

He was tall. A lot taller than me. And even in my heels I had to stand on my tiptoes. I expected a brutal tug in my hair, but his hands were a gentle slide.

He waited for me to give over. Waited for me to give him my permission. And his lips slid away from mine. His gaze burrowed deep into my eyes.

I nodded.

Yes. God, please, yes.

What happened next was more than I expected, a brutal and harsh slamming back of his lips to mine with a deep groan. His lips owned me. Not just devoured, but completely *consumed* me until I had no breath that he didn't allow.

His hands were gentle in my hair, but commanding. I knew exactly how he wanted me to move my head. I knew exactly the response he demanded from me. He led, and I followed. It was either that or be left behind. Jump off the ride, never get to experience this.

I had thought about Bridge Edgerton kissing me since I met him when I was ten years old. There was something about that lush, cruel mouth that evoked images of stolen kisses and whispered poetry. He was so stiff, aloof. But there was something inherently sensual about the way he moved, and if you could get him to smile, the man was a knockout. You had no choice but to stare at his sheer beauty. He looked like every tortured hero you'd ever been told about. But in that moment, I was the one being tortured.

My body was on fire. Straining, needing what only he could give. But instead of giving it to me, his tongue slid over mine, coaxing, teasing, owning. Leaving a wake that no one dared to follow.

One hand slid over my shoulders, molding the curve of my waist, over my arse and then pulling me close. And I could feel him. The steely, rigid length of his erection pressing against my abdomen. I shivered.

Holy hell.

All my mates talked about sex non-stop. It's what we did. We were fascinated, curious, scared, anticipatory. Because none of us had had any.

But the way Bridge was kissing me was a prelude. Maybe not tonight. Maybe not tomorrow, but one day, Bridge Edgerton was going to be inside me. And I was going to be happy about it and just a little bit terrified. Because, Christ, what was pressing against me was never, ever, *ever* going to fit.

But God, did I want him to try, because something low in my belly was pulling taut and tight and tingling and it warmed my skin. I needed it. I didn't even know why. But I knew I needed it from him.

He growled again against my lips. And his hips moved in a small circular motion that made me want to climb him.

I couldn't stop. I needed it. I followed suit, and he growled, his palms squeezing my arse. Bringing me tighter up against him. And then, just as I was getting into the rhythm, just as something was building inside me, something I couldn't name but wanted so desperately that I would have sold my soul to have it...

He pulled back. Lips swollen, eyes wide, breath tearing out of his chest in ragged pants, he glowered at me as if this was my fault. And then his cool mask slipped over his expression and he stepped back. "That shouldn't have happened."

I was too dazed to think, too tired, too dizzy to focus.

But then it occurred to me what he'd said. "I don't understand. Why would you say that?"

"Let's go. You need to get in the cab."

I blinked up at him. "The hell I do. You'll explain to me what the hell you mean. And first of all—"

I didn't get to finish what I was saying. Because before I knew it, his hands were on me again, and my heart leapt for joy.

But then he picked me up, flipped me over his shoulder, and carried me out of the little garden. Next thing I knew, his sharp, shrill whistle sounded, and then we were moving again, and a taxi pulled up.

He and the driver exchanged words, and he handed him some money. Then he opened the back door of the car, placed me inside, and closed the door with him on the other side.

I tried to roll down the window, but it didn't roll. So I knocked on the window, and he shook his head. He walked around the car and through the window from the driver's side of the taxi, he said, "You know where to take her."

"Bridge, what are you doing?"

"I'll see you around, Emma."

As the taxi drove away, I stared at the silhouette of Bridge Edgerton as he walked away from me.

Forever.

Continue Bridge and Emma's story in **London Bridge** ...

Thank you for reading BRIDGE OF LOVE!

Bridge Edgerton has only ever wanted one woman. One

little problem. She hates him. But he's sworn to protect her, so he can never have her.

Read *London Bridge!*

Read the STUNNING EDGE of your SEAT romance, that Sierra Simone calls, "...A delicious story of **secrets and revenge.**"

*It began with **betrayal**.*
*And ended in **murder**.*

She was never supposed to cross my path.
*She was never supposed to know about the **Currency of Secrets** or the **Oaths of Blood**.*

My so-called brothers killed my friend. *I intend to make them pay. And before it's over, I'll bend all the rules of morality, decency and legality. I will borrow and steal to set the scales right.*

My name is Ben Covington and I know my sins.

Read BIG BEN now!
"...a d**ramatic, suspenseful and amazing read**

that you just can't put down. I loved it!"——**Goodreads Reviewer**

Meet a cocky, billionaire prince that goes undercover in **Cheeky Royal** He's a prince with a secret to protect. The last distraction he can afford is his gorgeous as sin new neighbor. His secrets could get them killed, but still, he can't stay away...

Read Cheeky Royal for FREE now!

Turn the page for an excerpt from Cheeky Royal...

Continue Reading Bridge & Emma

Emma

It had taken me six weeks to get back to bloody London.

I was in New York with my mother when I got the note. The reminder that my work wasn't done.

Francis Middleton is the worst of them. You cannot let him walk.

A year ago, this journey had started with a note just like this. Printed on heavy ivory card stock. That message had pointed me to the Elite, the secret society my brother would have been part of. The same secret society that had been responsible for his death. I'd gone to the only people I could for help. Ben Covington, East Hale, Drew Wilcox, and Bridge Edgerton. My brother's closest friends.

They'd promised me retribution.

But now at the finish line, things had stalled. And instead of telling me something, *anything*, they'd gone silent and shuffled me away from London... presumably for my own safety.

But one, I didn't need saving. And two, this note had found me in New York, so how safe had I been really?

East, Ben, and Bridge hadn't been kidding when they said they'd take care of everything. Bridge and the boys had bought my mother's house, regardless of what it was actually worth, just like that and put it wholly in her name. As if it was nothing. And then they forced me back to the States with my mother. Which, God, I loved my mother, and it was good to see her. But it wasn't for them to decide who I was or what I wanted to do. I wasn't a child anymore.

Hell, they'd even gotten me a dream job. But the whole time I was there, not a single word came about my brother, his killers, or what they were doing about the final one.

Which meant I had to take matters into my own hands. Which meant returning under cover of night so to speak... if I didn't want the four assholes of the apocalypse to send me right back to my mother like a recalcitrant child.

I'd need to fly under the radar. And not tip them off that I was back. While I was still doing marketing work for my old company remotely, I'd also need a job here in London. I'd been careful though. My passport had been stamped in France, and then I'd taken the train. Immigration would mark that they'd seen me come through, but Bridge wouldn't have access to that. East's fiancé, Nyla Kincade might with her Interpol connections, but I didn't think she'd rat me out like that.

The point was, they didn't own me. I was the one who'd gotten them started on this vengeance thing to begin with, and now they wanted to kick me out of it?

Toby was my brother. I deserved vengeance just as much as they did. I deserved to be part of the takedown, but they'd tried to keep me out of it.

Well, not anymore.

I'd been watching Bridge for the last two weeks, and what I'd heard was true. He and Mina had broken up, so he'd been rambling around that house by himself. Sometimes, when he'd work late, he'd stay at his suite at the hotel. I'd been watching the house all day, and he still hadn't returned, so it meant he was very likely going to stay at his suite.

I parked my car and walked the block up to the house in Belgravia. I smiled to the security guard, who I recognized from the last couple of times I'd been there, and he said, "Oh, Miss Varma."

I flashed him a winning smile that said I belonged there. "Yes, I'm here to see Mr. Edgerton. Is he here?"

He shook his head. "No. Not according to the logs. He won't be returning this evening."

Even better. I would grab his laptop, have a quick look, and I'd be in and out before he even knew anything. Sure, he'd see me on the security cameras eventually, and the guard would tell him I'd been there, but I'd be long gone by then. And I'd stay hidden.

"Would I be able to go in? The last time I was here I left something behind, and I sort of need it now. I have the code."

The furrows of his brow eased before they even started to form. "Oh, you know the code. Please type it in here, and you may enter."

That was the thing about being forgotten. While we'd been meeting, we all had our own personal codes so as not to deal with security every single time we came. Even though Mina's had been changed, there was no reason to change any of ours. Bridge had simply forgotten that I had access to his house. *Amateur.*

I typed in my code and then said a little prayer to every god I could think of. I'd been raised Catholic, but I hadn't darkened the door of the church in at least fifteen years. But now, it seemed like as good a time as any to find my faith. When the screen lit green, he nodded and pressed his own code to open the gate. "Just use the same code for the front door and you're good to go."

"Oh, excellent. I won't be but a minute."

I went in swiftly, as if I owned the joint. Bridge thought he was so slick in keeping me away from all of this, but what he didn't understand was that I would not sit back like a little woman. Toby would have expected me to be a hundred percent myself. And this was me being myself. Bridge Edgerton could kiss my ass. He'd been telling me what to do for years, but I was done with being controlled.

When I let myself in the house, a giddy sense of excitement tripped over my skin as his scent hit me. No longer was there a hint of femininity in the house. No bowls of potpourri, but the scent of sandalwood lingered in the expanse. It made a part of me deep inside clench. I loved that smell. Why did he have to smell so good? Honestly, he was a pure asshole, but he smelled like a fucking delight.

I thought back to that one kiss we'd shared when we were kids. Possibly the hottest kiss I'd ever had in my life. But he'd walked away, vowing to never touch me again, which was fine, because I had zero interest in being controlled for the rest of my life.

Liar.

A quick search of the house told me his laptop wasn't there. And that's what I fucking needed. There was a prick at the back of my eyes as I resisted the urge to cry. No. All this meant was that I was going to have to go to his suite in the hotel. And that would take a little more ingenuity, but I wasn't giving up. Bridge Edgerton had another think coming if he thought I was just going to sit back and do as I was told.

* * *

Bridge

I hadn't been staying at the house lately. Suddenly, it seemed I had turned into Ben before Livy came along. I had a big fancy house and refused to stay in it. I'd only opted to stay in the house tonight because I had a meeting on this side of town in the morning. But I'd avoided my own staff by slipping in through the back during a shift change.

I wasn't going to subject any of them to my mood.

What the fuck was wrong with me?

What's wrong is that the woman you thought you loved was hired by your fucking father.

It was like the old man would never cease to be a thorn in my side.

He wanted nothing to do with me publicly, but he still wanted to control me.

I grabbed the pillow and rolled over in the bed again. I was hot. Tight. Itchy. I just wanted out of my own fucking skin. Sleep was so far off in the horizon, I felt like giving up. I was in the process of rolling over again when I heard something in the other room.

What the fuck was that? It sounded like a light scraping noise.

I sat still, calmed my breathing, and waited. That was definitely a muttered curse coming from the living room of the suite.

Fucking Christ, that was the last thing I needed. There had been a time when I'd been a different person, rough around the edges, the one that was likely to end up in jail. Angry all of the time, and I was angry for reasons I couldn't control. I'd smoothed those rough edges and made something of my life, but now, it seemed like the old me needed to come to the forefront or something very bad was going to happen.

Under my bedside table, I reached for the one thing vested in my former life that I kept handy. The switch blade was just as I remembered it. Cold. Delicate. Deadly.

Just like Mina.

I shoved the thoughts of my ex out of my head. I didn't want to think about her and all her lies.

I sprung up out of bed. As usual, I slept commando, so I padded over to the closet and eased the bottom drawer open on the far left. I took a pair of boxers from it and tugged them on. If I was about to have a fight, there was no need to have the lads flying about uncovered.

Luckily, I slept with my door slightly ajar, so easing into the living room didn't cause any unwanted sound. Then I saw it. The shadow in the study, going through my things.

What the fuck? How had anyone gotten in here?

My feet moved of their own volition. My rational brain was chirping up with things like, 'Call security. You are closer to the door than to the study, so just leave.' Or the oh so helpful, 'At least put a fucking shirt on.'

No, I wasn't going to do any of those things. I was going to find out who the fuck was in my suite.

The study door was open, and I saw someone dressed in all black. One of my fucking employees? I could play this scenario one of two ways. I could approach, turn on the lights, and ask them what the fuck they thought they were doing, or I could jump them. I was irritated enough that option two seemed excellent to me.

With a step-over-step motion, I slid against the window to the living room. And then, it was easy.

One arm in a choke hold, the other pressing the knife against the jugular, leaning close. The person was small, delicate. A light floral scent hit my nostrils and I inhaled deep. A woman? The slight stature, the curves, definitely a woman. Not Mina though. She was shorter and not as strong. The woman in my arms delivered a half decent elbow to my ribs. Enough to make me grind my teeth.

And why did she smell so fucking familiar?

My fucking dick didn't seem to know any better. This wasn't some game with a girl who liked it rough. This was deadly serious. But God, why did she smell... and then I knew why. I whipped my intruder around so fast that she squeaked, and with my hand on her throat, I backed her up against the wall and placed the knife to her jugular again.

"What the fuck are you doing here, Emma?"

* * *

Thank you for reading BRIDGE OF LOVE!

Bridge Edgerton has only ever wanted one woman. One little problem. She hates him. But he's sworn to protect her, so he can never have her.

Read *London Bridge!*

Read the STUNNING EDGE of your SEAT romance, that Sierra Simone calls, "...A delicious story of **secrets and revenge.**"

*It began with **betrayal**.*
*And ended in **murder**.*

She was never supposed to cross my path.
*She was never supposed to know about the **Currency of Secrets** or the **Oaths of Blood**.*

My so-called brothers killed my friend. I intend to make them pay. And before it's over, I'll bend all the rules of morality, decency and legality. I will borrow and steal to set the scales right.

My name is Ben Covington and I know my sins.

Read BIG BEN now!
"...a d**ramatic, suspenseful and amazing read** that you just can't put down. I loved it!"———*Goodreads Reviewer*

Meet a cocky, billionaire prince that goes undercover in **Cheeky Royal** He's a prince with a secret to protect. The last distraction he can afford is his gorgeous as sin new neighbor. His secrets could get them killed, but still, he can't stay away...

Read Cheeky Royal for FREE now!

Turn the page for an excerpt from Cheeky Royal...

Also from Nana Malone
Cheeky Royal

"You make a really good model. I'm sure dozens of artists have volunteered to paint you before."
He shook his head. "Not that I can recall. Why? Are you offering?"

I grinned. "I usually do nudes." Why did I say that? It wasn't true. Because you're hoping he'll volunteer as tribute.

He shrugged then reached behind his back and pulled his shirt up, tugged it free, and tossed it aside. "How is this for nude?"

Fuck. Me. I stared for a moment, mouth open and looking

like an idiot. Then, well, I snapped a picture. Okay fine, I snapped several. "Uh, that's a start."

He ran a hand through his hair and tussled it, so I snapped several of that. These were romance-cover gold. Getting into it, he started posing for me, making silly faces. I got closer to him, snapping more close-ups of his face. That incredible face.

Then suddenly he went deadly serious again, the intensity in his eyes going harder somehow, sharper. Like a razor. "You look nervous. I thought you said you were used to nudes."

I swallowed around the lump in my throat. "Yeah, at school whenever we had a model, they were always nude. I got used to it."

He narrowed his gaze. "Are you sure about that?"
Shit. He could tell. "Yeah, I am. It's just a human form. Male. Female. No big deal."

His lopsided grin flashed, and my stomach flipped. Stupid traitorous body...and damn him for being so damn good looking. I tried to keep the lens centered on his face, but I had to get several of his abs, for you know...research.

But when his hand rubbed over his stomach and then slid to the button on his jeans, I gasped, "What are you doing?"
"Well, you said you were used doing nudes. Will that make you more comfortable as a photographer?"

I swallowed again, unable to answer, wanting to know what he was doing, how far he would go. And how far would I go?

The button popped, and I swallowed the sawdust in my mouth. I snapped a picture of his hands.

Well yeah, and his abs. So sue me. He popped another button, giving me a hint of the forbidden thing I couldn't have. I kept snapping away. We were locked in this odd, intimate game of chicken. I swung the lens up to capture his face. His gaze was slightly hooded. His lips parted... turned on. I stepped back a step to capture all of him. His jeans loose, his feet bare. Sitting on the stool, leaning back slightly and giving me the sex face, because that's what it was—God's honest truth—the sex face. And I was a total goner.

"You're not taking pictures, Len." His voice was barely above a whisper.

"Oh, sorry." I snapped several in succession. Full body

shots, face shots, torso shots. There were several torso shots. I wanted to fully capture what was happening.

He unbuttoned another button, taunting me, tantalizing me. Then he reached into his jeans, and my gaze snapped to meet his. I wanted to say something. Intervene in some way...help maybe...ask him what he was doing. But I couldn't. We were locked in a game that I couldn't break free from. Now I wanted more. I wanted to know just how far he would go.

Would he go nude? Or would he stay in this half-undressed state, teasing me, tempting me to do the thing that I shouldn't do?

I snapped more photos, but this time I was close. I was looking down on him with the camera, angling so I could see his perfectly sculpted abs as they flexed. His hand was inside his jeans. From the bulge, I knew he was touching himself. And then I snapped my gaze up to his face. Sebastian licked his lip, and I captured the moment that tongue met flesh.

Heat flooded my body, and I pressed my thighs together to abate the ache. At that point, I was just snapping photos, completely in the zone, wanting to see what he might do next.

"Len..."

"Sebastian." My voice was so breathy I could barely get it past my lips.

"Do you want to come closer?"

"I--I think maybe I'm close enough?"

His teeth grazed his bottom lip. "Are you sure about that? I have another question for you."

I snapped several more images, ranging from face shots to shoulders, to torso. Yeah, I also went back to the hand-around-his-dick thing because...wow. "Yeah? Go ahead."

"Why didn't you tell me about your boyfriend 'til now?"

Oh shit. "I—I'm not sure. I didn't think it mattered. It sort of feels like we're supposed to be friends." Lies all lies.

He stood, his big body crowding me. "Yeah, friends..."

I swallowed hard. I couldn't bloody think with him so close. His scent assaulted me, sandalwood and something that was pure Sebastian wrapped around me, making me weak. Making me tingle as I inhaled his scent. Heat throbbed between my thighs, even as my knees went weak. "Sebastian, wh—what are you doing?"

"

Proving to you that we're not friends. Will you let me?"

He was asking my permission. I knew what I wanted to say. I understood what was at stake. But then he raised his hand

and traced his knuckles over my cheek, and a whimper escaped.

His voice went softer, so low when he spoke, his words were more like a rumble than anything intelligible. "Is that you telling me to stop?"

Seriously, there were supposed to be words. There were. But somehow I couldn't manage them, so like an idiot I shook my head.

His hand slid into my curls as he gently angled my head. When he leaned down, his lips a whisper from mine, he whispered, "This is all I've been thinking about."

Read Cheeky Royal for FREE now!

About Nana Malone

Wall Street Journal & USA Today Bestselling author, Nana Malone writes Sexy Feel-Good Romance and loves all things romance and adventure.

That love started with a tattered romantic suspense she "borrowed" from her cousin. It was a sultry summer afternoon in Ghana, and Nana was a precocious thirteen. She's been in love with kick butt heroines ever since. With her overactive imagination, and channeling her inner Buffy, it was only a matter a time before she started creating her own characters.

9 781734 135145